SPIKE

written and illustrated by

Paulette Bogan

G. P. Putnam's Sons   New York

Copyright © 1998 by Paulette Bogan
All rights reserved. This book, or parts thereof,
may not be reproduced in any form without
permission in writing from the publisher.
G. P. Putnam's Sons, a division of The Putnam & Grosset Group,
200 Madison Avenue, New York, NY 10016.
G. P. Putnam's Sons, Reg. U.S. Pat. & Tm. Off.
Published simultaneously in Canada
Printed and bound in Singapore.
Designed by Marikka Tamura. Text set in Clichee Bold
Library of Congress Cataloging-in-Publication Data
Bogan, Paulette. Spike/
written and illustrated by Paulette Bogan. p. cm.
Summary: Tired and bored with his life as a dog,
Spike leaves home to try doing what other animals do.
[1. Dogs—Fiction. 2. Animals—Fiction. 3. Self-acceptance—Fiction.]
I. Title. PZ7.B6357835Sp 1998 [E]—dc21 96-45328 CIP AC
ISBN 0-399-23163-3
1 3 5 7 9 10 8 6 4 2
First Impression

Special thanks to

Mom & Dad,
Charlie,
&
Pat Cummings

Spike had been a dog for six years now.
All he ever did was run and jump and play
Frisbee. It was so boring! He wanted to be
someone else. ANYONE else!!

One day Shannon, the little girl who
owned him, left the back gate open.
Spike saw his big chance and crept away.

Soon he came upon Howard the horse.
Howard could gallop really fast
and give people rides.
"NEIGH," said Howard as he sped past.

"Ouch!" said Spike. He couldn't even stand up with a rider on his back. "I'm not a very good horse."

Next he saw Rebecca the bird. She could
soar through the air and sing sweetly.
"TWEET, TWEET, TWEET," sang Rebecca.

"Watch out belooow!" yelled Spike.
He fell flat on his face.
"I'm not a very good bird."

When Spike saw Chelsey the chicken,
he couldn't believe his eyes.
She could lay eggs!
"BUCK, BUCK, BUCK," clucked Chelsey.

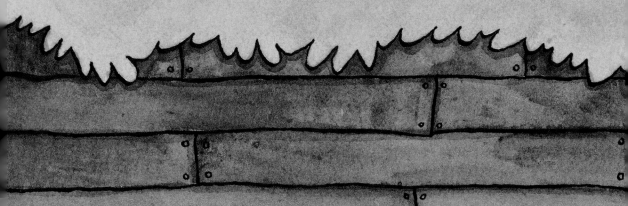

"YEEECH!" said Spike.
He broke all the eggs when he sat on them.

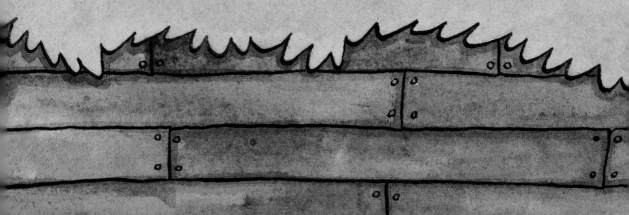

Soon Spike came across Jeffrey the fish.
WOW, he could jump out of the water
and dive really deep.
"SPLISH, SPLASH," went Jeffrey.

"Brrr," whined Spike. He felt wet and cold.
"I'm not a very good fish."

Spike was so sad, he decided to head home.

Shannon was sitting in the yard crying.
She was so sad that Spike was gone.

Spike ran up and gave Shannon a big kiss.
"SLURP!" He forgot how good it felt
to make her smile.